The Cat
and the Fiddle
A Treasury of Nursery Rhymes

For my very good friend, Claire Carlile
and for Billy, the beautiful golden dog

JANETTA OTTER-BARRY BOOKS

Text and Illustrations copyright © Jackie Morris 2011
The right of Jackie Morris to be identified as the Author and Illustrator of this Work has been
asserted by her in accordance with the Copyright, Designs and Patent Act, 1988 (United Kingdom).

First published in Great Britain and in the USA in 2011 by
Frances Lincoln Children's Books, 74-77 White Lion Street
London N1 9PF
www.franceslincoln.com

First paperback published in Great Britain in 2014 and in the USA in 2015

A CIP catalogue record for this book is available from the British Library.

ISBN 978-1-84780-458-7

Illustrated with watercolours

Printed in China

1 3 5 7 9 8 6 4 2

The Cat
and the Fiddle

A Treasury of Nursery Rhymes

Jackie Morris

F

FRANCES LINCOLN
CHILDREN'S BOOKS

Jack be nimble, Jack be quick,
Jack jump over the candlestick.

Contents

Ride a Cock-Horse

Ride a cock-horse to Banbury Cross,
To see a fine lady upon a white horse;

With rings on her fingers and bells on her toes,
She shall have music wherever she goes.

I Saw a Ship a-Sailing

I saw a ship a-sailing,
A-sailing on the sea,
And oh, but it was laden
With pretty things for me.

There were raisins in the cabins,
And apples in the hold;
The sails were made of silk,
And the masts were all of gold.

The four-and-twenty sailors
That stood upon the decks
Were four-and-twenty white mice
With chains around their necks.

The captain was a duck, a duck,
With a jacket on his back,
And when the ship began to move
The captain said, Quack! Quack!

Hickory, Dickory, Dock

Hickory, dickory, dock,
The mouse ran up the clock.
The clock struck one,
The mouse ran down,
Hickory, dickory, dock.

Cupboard Cat

A B C
Tumble down D
The cat's in the cupboard
And he can't see me!

Lavender's Blue

Lavender's blue, dilly, dilly,
Lavender's green.
When I am king, dilly, dilly,
You shall be queen.

Lilies are White

Lilies are white, rosemary's green,
When I am king, you will be queen.

There Was an Old Woman

There was an old woman tossed up in a basket,
Seventeen times as high as the moon;
Where she was going I couldn't but ask it,
For in her hand she carried a broom.

Old woman, old woman, old woman, said I,
Where are you going to, up so high?
To brush the cobwebs off the sky!
May I go with you? Aye, by-and-by.

How Many Miles to Babylon?

How many miles to Babylon?
Three score miles and ten.
Can I get there by candle-light?

Yes, and back again.
If your heels are nimble and light,
You will get there by candle-light.

The Lion and the Unicorn

The lion and the unicorn
Were fighting for the crown;
The lion beat the unicorn
All about the town.

Some gave them white bread
And some gave them brown;
Some gave them plum cake
And drummed them out of town.

A Swarm of Bees in May

A swarm of bees in May
Is worth a load of hay.

A swarm of bees in June
Is worth a silver spoon.

Ladybird, Ladybird

Ladybird, ladybird,
Fly away home,
Your house is on fire
And your children all gone,
All except one
And that's little Ann,
For she crept under
The frying pan.

A swarm of bees in July
Is not even worth a fly.

Spring

March winds and April showers
Bring forth May flowers.

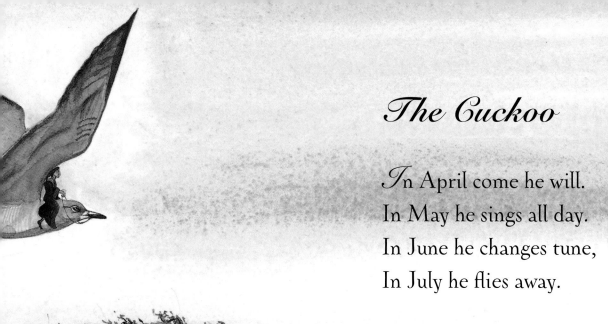

The Cuckoo

In April come he will.
In May he sings all day.
In June he changes tune,
In July he flies away.

The First of May

The fair maid who, on the first of May,
Goes to the fields at the break of day,
And washes in the dew of the hawthorn tree,
Will ever after handsome be.

All the Pretty Little Horses

Hush a bye, don't you cry,
Go to sleep, my little baby.
When you wake, you will have a cake
And all the pretty little horses.

Black and bay and dappled and grey,
Coach and six white horses.

Pop! Goes the Weasel!

Half a pound of tuppenny rice,
Half a pound of treacle,
That's the way the money goes,
Pop! goes the weasel!

Up and down the City Road,
In and out of the Eagle.
That's the way the money goes!
Pop! goes the weasel!

Four-and-Twenty Tailors

Four-and-twenty tailors
Went to catch a snail,
The bravest one amongst them
Dared not touch her tail;

She put out her horns
Like a little Kyloe cow,
Run, tailors, run,
Or she'll catch you even now.

Twinkle, Twinkle, Little Star

Twinkle, twinkle, little star,
How I wonder what you are!
Up above the world so high,
Like a diamond in the sky.
Twinkle, twinkle, little star,
How I wonder what you are!

To the Bat

Bat, bat, fly under my hat,
And I'll give you a slice of bacon;
And when I bake, I'll bake you a cake,
If I'm not mistaken.

Sing a Song of Sixpence

Sing a song of sixpence,
A pocketful of rye;
Four-and-twenty blackbirds
Baked in a pie.

When the pie was opened
The birds began to sing;
Wasn't that a dainty dish
To set before a king?

The king was in the counting house
Counting out his money;
The queen was in the parlour
Eating bread and honey.

The maid was in the garden
Hanging out the clothes,
When down came a blackbird
And pecked off her nose.

Pudding String

Sing, sing, what shall I sing?
The cat's run away with the pudding string.

Do, do, what shall I do?
The cat has bitten it quite in two.

I Love Little Pussy

I love little pussy,
Her coat is so warm,
And if I don't hurt her
She'll do me no harm.

So I'll not pull her tail,
Nor drive her away,
But pussy and I
Very gently will play.

Pussy Cat, Pussy Cat

Pussy cat, pussy cat,
Where have you been?
I've been to London
To visit the queen.
Pussy cat, pussy cat, what did you there?
I frightened a little mouse
Under her chair.

Jumping Joan

Here am I, little Jumping Joan,
When nobody's with me, I'm all alone.

Little Thomas Tittlemouse

Little Thomas Tittlemouse
Lived in a little house.
He caught fishes
In other men's ditches.

My Black Hen

Higglety-pigglety, my black hen,
She lays eggs for gentlemen,
Sometimes nine and sometimes ten,
Higglety-pigglety, my black hen.

Cock a Doodle Doo

Cock a doodle doo!
My dame has lost her shoe,
My master's lost his fiddling stick
And doesn't know what to do.

Baa, Baa, Black Sheep

Baa, baa, black sheep,
Have you any wool?
Yes, sir, yes, sir,
Three bags full;

One for the master,
And one for the dame,
And one for the little boy
Who lives down the lane.

Daffy-Down Dilly

Daffy-Down Dilly has come up to town
In a yellow petticoat and a green gown.

Hark, Hark

Hark, hark,
The dogs do bark,
The beggars are coming to town;
Some in rags,
And some in tags,
And one in a velvet gown.

Tom, He Was a Piper's Son

Tom, he was a piper's son.
He learned to play when he was young.
But the only tune that he could play
Was over the hills and far away.

To Market

To market, to market,
To buy a fat pig.
Home again, home again,
Jiggety jig.

Little Bo-Peep

Little Bo-Peep has lost her sheep,
And doesn't know where to find them;
Leave them alone, and they'll come home,
Bringing their tails behind them.

Grey Goose

Grey goose and gander,
Waft your wings together,
And carry the good king's daughter
Over the one-strand river.

Hey Diddle, Diddle

Hey diddle, diddle,
The cat and the fiddle,
The cow jumped over the moon;
The little dog laughed
To see such sport,
And the dish ran away with the spoon.

I Had a Little Nut Tree

I had a little nut tree, nothing would it bear
But a silver nutmeg and a golden pear.
The King of Spain's daughter came to visit me,
And all for the sake of my little nut tree.
I skipped over water, I danced over sea,
And all the birds in the air couldn't catch me.

The Hart and the Hare

The hart, he loves the high wood,
The hare, she loves the hill;
The knight, he loves his bright sword,
And the lady loves her will.

The Bed is Too Small

The bed is too small for my tired head,
Bring me a hill soft with trees;
Tuck a cloud up under my chin,
Lord, blow the moon out, please.

Baby's Bed's a Silver Moon

Baby's bed's a silver moon
Sailing o'er the sky,
Sailing o'er the sea of sleep,
While the stars go by.

Sail, baby, sail,
Far across the sea.
And don't forget to come
Back home again to me.

Baby's fishing for a dream,
Fishing near and far,
Her line a silver moonbeam is,
Her bait a silver star.

Sail, baby, sail,
Far across the sea.
But don't forget to come
Back home again to me.

MORE BESTSELLING PICTURE BOOKS FROM JACKIE MORRIS
FOR FRANCES LINCOLN CHILDREN'S BOOKS

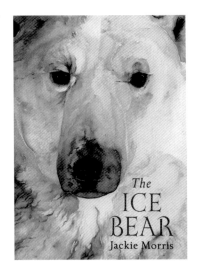

The Ice Bear

Long ago in the icy lands of the far north, a hunter and his wife cared for an orphaned bear-child. But when the child wanders off, there are consequences. Set in the pristine regions of the Arctic, Jackie Morris's captivating illustrations and lyrical text remind us that we are caretakers of wild creatures, and that our actions affect the future.

"One of the most wonderful picture books of the year."
– *Amanda Craig, The Times*

The Snow Leopard

Jackie Morris's poetic text weaves the spirit of nature into a universal myth for our time. Set against the stunning landscapes of the Himalayas, her beautiful illustrations of the endangered snow leopard offer a message of hope at a time when many of the world's wildest places are being worn away.

"Vivid watercolour illustrations that meld ink-brush abstraction and subtle detail into a gorgeous fantasy."
– *New York Times*

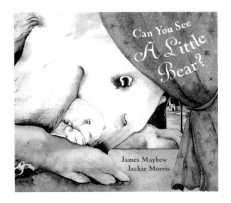

Can You See a Little Bear?

A sumptuous look-and-find book where children can follow simple clues in the read-aloud nursery rhyme verse to find the Little Bear on each page.

"This look-and-find journey through a series of ultra-colourful settings in different countries is simply astonishing." – *Independent*

Frances Lincoln titles are available from all good bookshops.
You can also buy books and find out more about your favourite titles,
authors and illustrators on our website: www.franceslincoln.com